Current Hits

for Students

7 Graded Selections for Early Intermediate Pianists

Arranged by

Carol Matz

MW00448974

Students of all ages love playing popular pieces by their favorite recording artists. This collection includes accessible arrangements of pop hits by Katy Perry, Lady Gaga, Justin Bieber, Scotty McCreery, Paramore, Christina Perri and Michael Bublé. The arrangements are "teacher friendly," while remaining faithful to the sound of the original recording. In this early-intermediate collection, 16th notes are avoided, key signatures are limited to no more than one flat or two sharps, and $\frac{6}{8}$ time and swing rhythm are introduced.

Produced by
Alfred Music Publishing Co., Inc.
P.O. Box 10003
Van Nuys, CA 91410-0003
alfred.com

Printed in USA.

ISBN-10: 0-7390-8630-8
ISBN-13: 978-0-7390-8630-8

FIREWORK

Words and Music by Katy Perry, Mikkel Eriksen,
Tor Erik Hermansen, Sandy Wilhelm and Ester Dean
Arranged by Carol Matz

no one seems to hear a thing. Do you know that there's still a chance for you?

'Cause there's a spark in you. You just got - ta ig - nite

the light and let it shine.

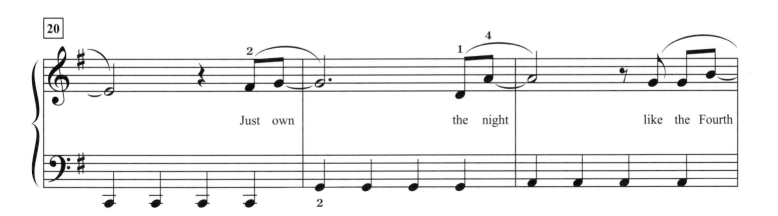

Just own the night like the Fourth

of Ju - ly. 'Cause, ba - by, you're a fi - re - work.

Come on, show 'em what you're worth. Make 'em go,

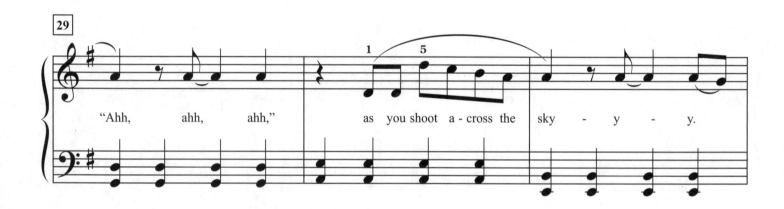

"Ahh, ahh, ahh," as you shoot a - cross the sky - y - y.

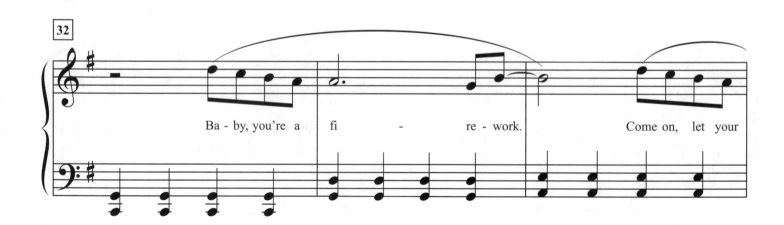

Ba - by, you're a fi - re - work. Come on, let your

col - ors burst. Make 'em go, "Ahh, ahh, ahh."

You're gon - na leave them all in awe, awe, awe.

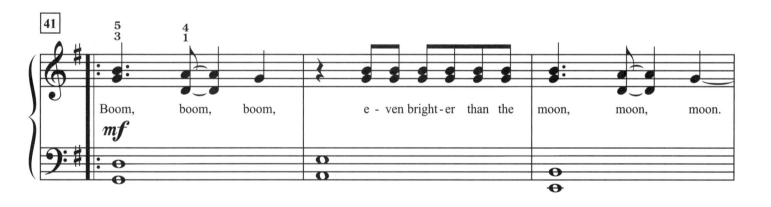

Boom, boom, boom, e - ven bright - er than the moon, moon, moon.

mf

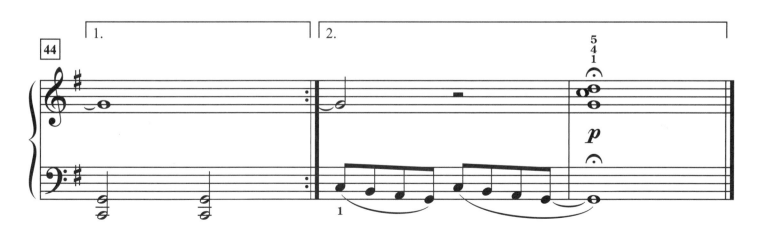

1.　　　　　2.

p

BORN THIS WAY

Words and Music by Fernando Garibay,
Stefani Germanotta, Jeppe Laursen and Paul Blair
Arranged by Carol Matz

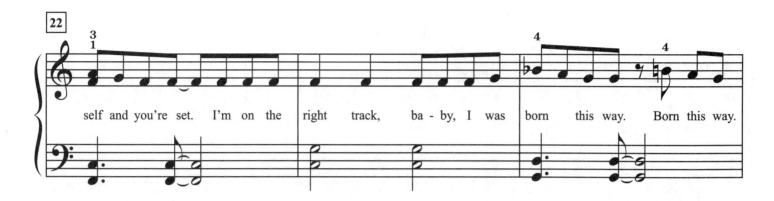

self and you're set. I'm on the right track, ba - by, I was born this way. Born this way.

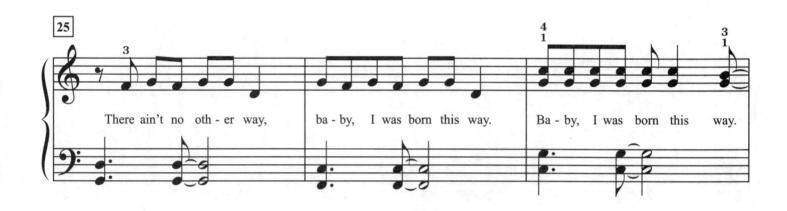

There ain't no oth - er way, ba - by, I was born this way. Ba - by, I was born this way.

Born this way. There ain't no oth - er way, ba - by, I was born this way.

Right track, ba - by, I was born this way, hey.

BABY

Words and Music by Terius Nash, Christopher Stewart,
Christine Flores, Christopher Bridges and Justin Bieber
Arranged by Carol Matz

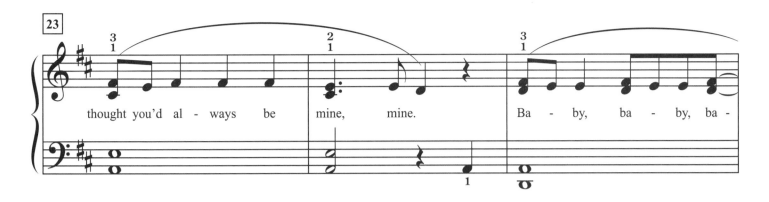

thought you'd al - ways be mine, mine. Ba - by, ba - by, ba -

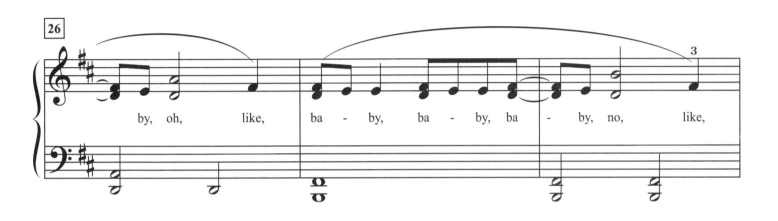

by, oh, like, ba - by, ba - by, ba - by, no, like,

ba - by, ba - by, ba - by, oh, thought you'd al - ways be

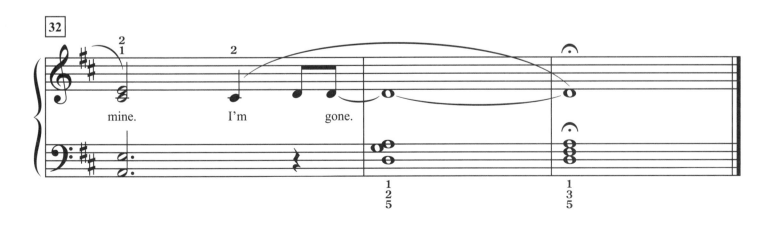

mine. I'm gone.

I LOVE YOU THIS BIG

Words and Music by Ronnie Jackson,
Brett James, Ester Dean and Jay Smith
Arranged by Carol Matz

by the way my heart starts pound - ing

when I look in - to your eyes.

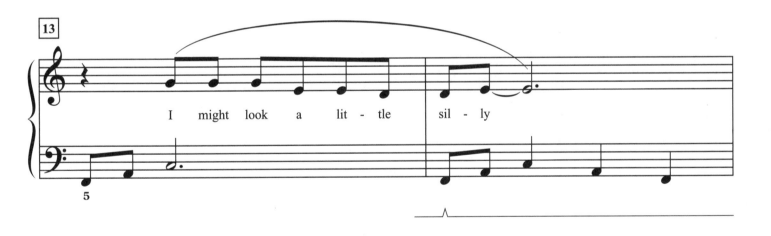

I might look a lit - tle sil - ly

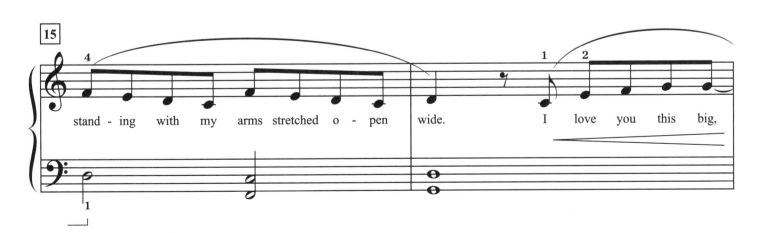

stand - ing with my arms stretched o - pen wide. I love you this big,

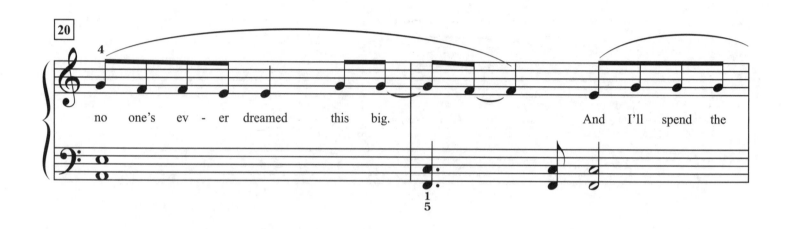

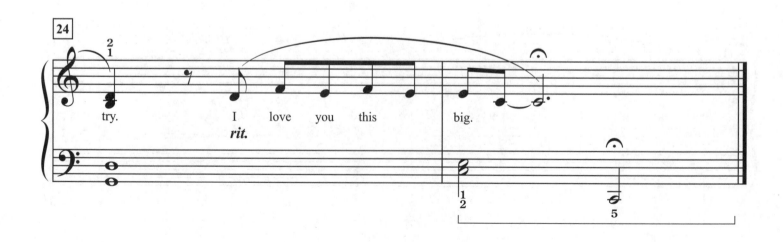

THE ONLY EXCEPTION

Words and Music by Hayley Williams and Josh Farro
Arranged by Carol Matz

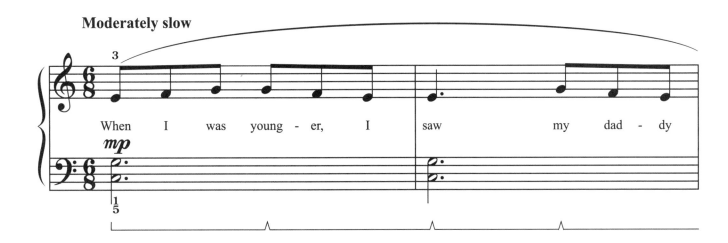

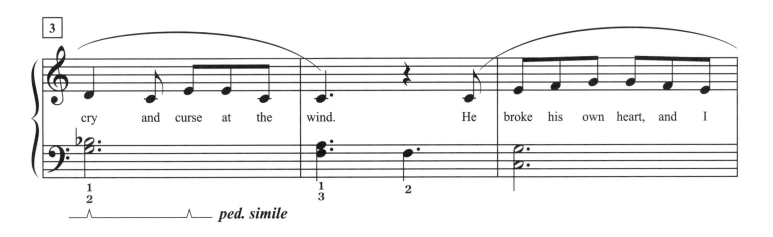

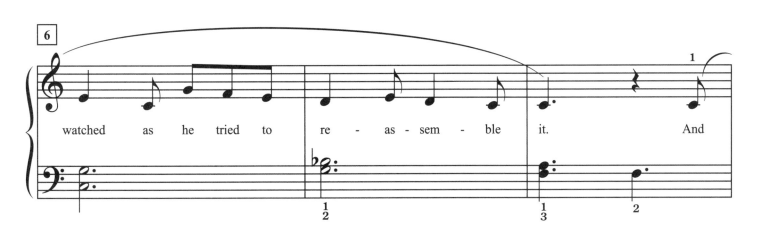

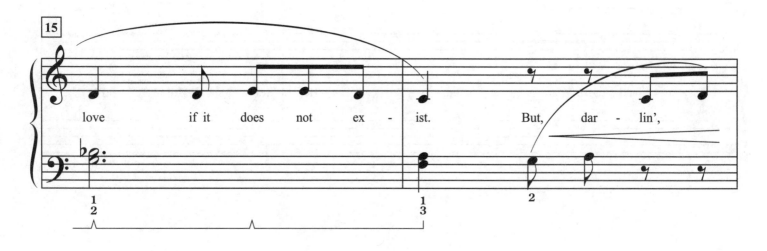

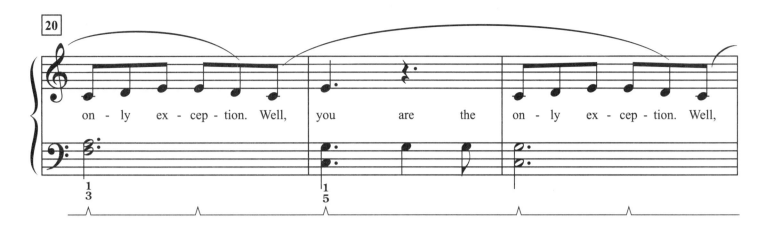

on - ly ex - cep - tion. Well, you are the on - ly ex - cep - tion. Well,

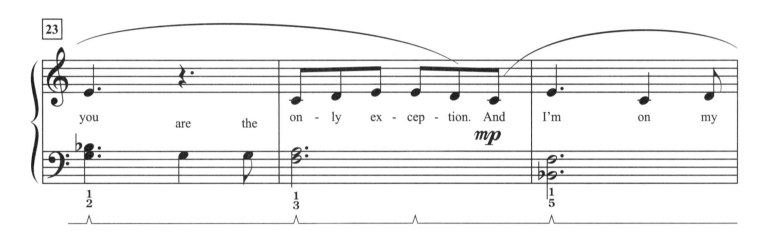

you are the on - ly ex - cep - tion. And I'm on my

mp

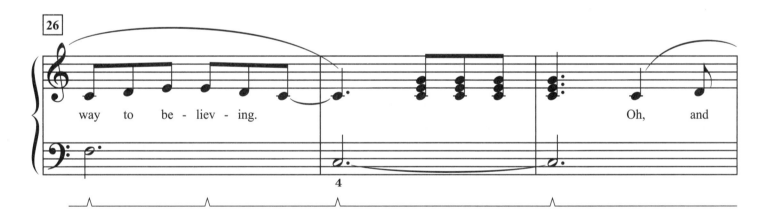

way to be - liev - ing. Oh, and

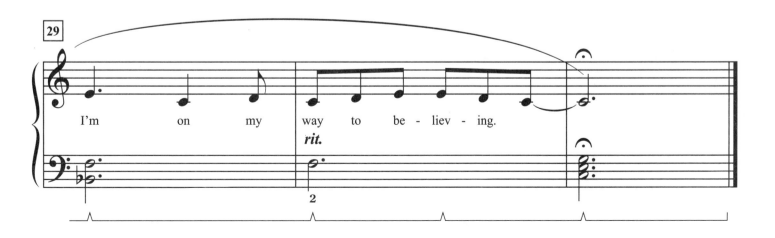

I'm on my way to be - liev - ing.

rit.

JAR OF HEARTS

Words and Music by Drew Lawrence,
Christina Perri and Barrett Yeretsian
Arranged by Carol Matz

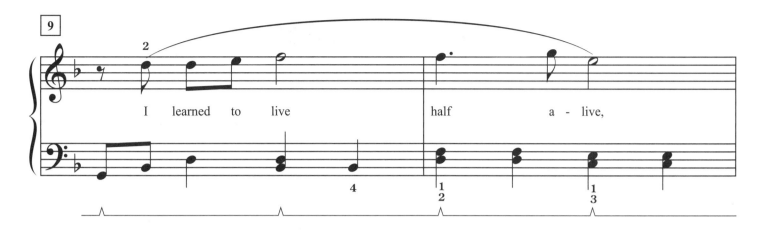

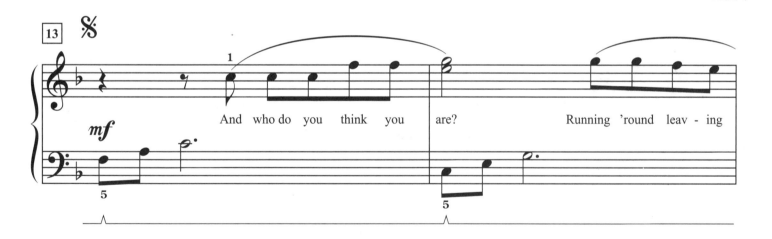

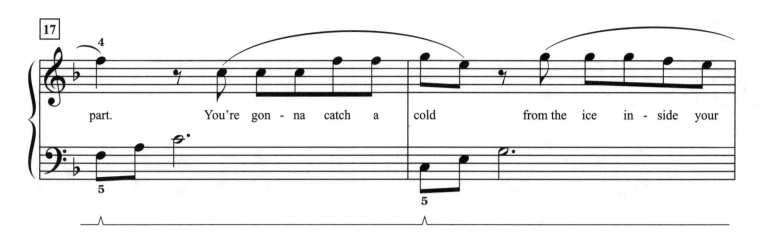

17

part. You're gon - na catch a cold from the ice in - side your

to Coda ⊕

19

soul, so don't come back for me. Who do you think you

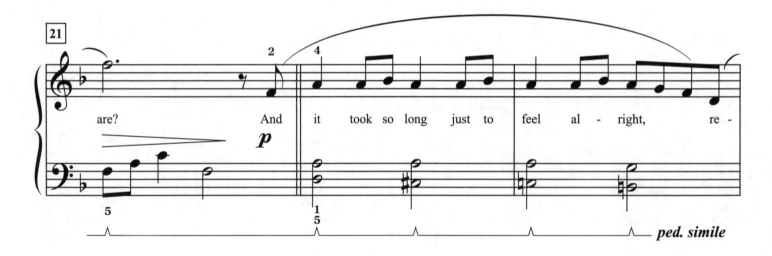

21

are? And it took so long just to feel al - right, re-

p

ped. simile

24

mem - ber how to put back the light in my eyes. I

mp

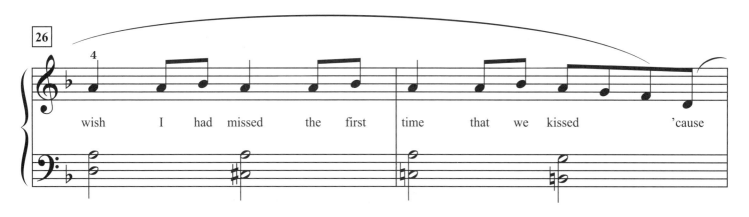

wish I had missed the first time that we kissed 'cause

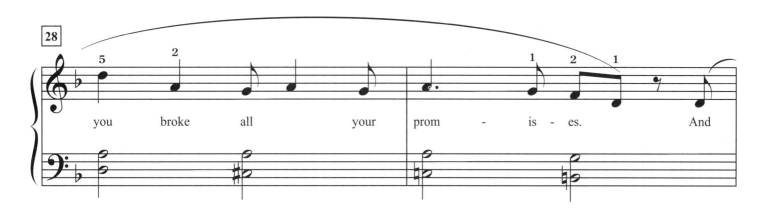

you broke all your prom - is - es. And

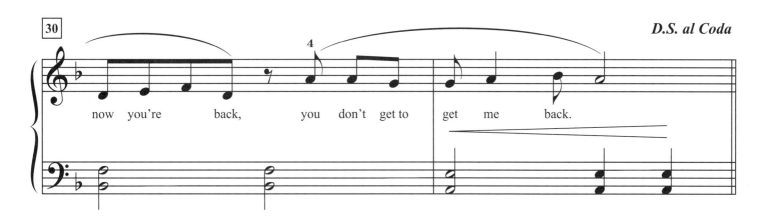

D.S. al Coda

now you're back, you don't get to get me back.

Coda

me. Who do you think you are?

rit. e dim.

$\boldsymbol{p}$

HAVEN'T MET YOU YET

Words and Music by Michael Bublé,
Alan Chang and Amy Foster
Arranged by Carol Matz

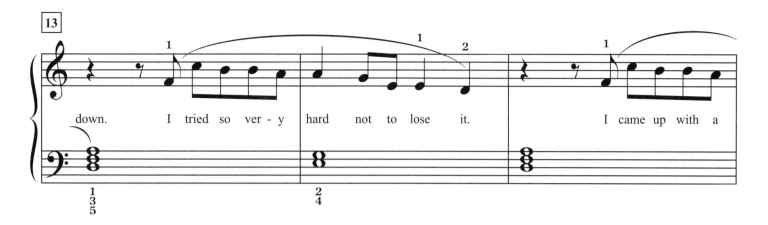

down. I tried so ver - y hard not to lose it. I came up with a

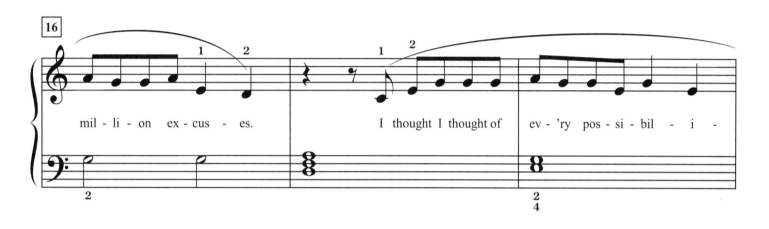

mil - li - on ex - cus - es. I thought I thought of ev - 'ry pos - si - bil - i -

ty. And I know some - day that it - 'll all turn out.

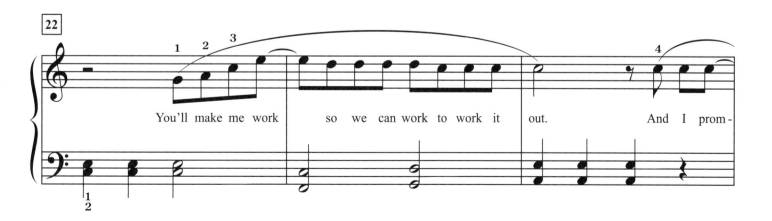

You'll make me work so we can work to work it out. And I prom -

ise you, kid, that I'll give so much more than I get. I

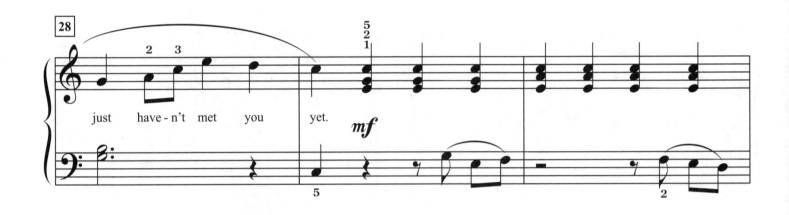

just have-n't met you yet. *mf*

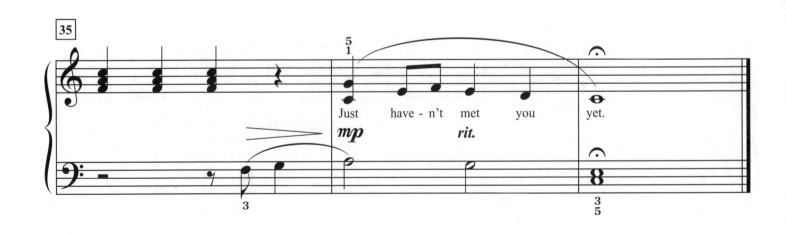

Just have-n't met you yet. *mp* *rit.*